What Civilization Is Not

Devajit Bhuyan

Ukiyoto Publishing

All global publishing rights are held by

Ukiyoto Publishing

Published in 2023

Content Copyright © Devajit Bhuyan

ISBN 9789360160739

All rights reserved.
No part of this publication may be reproduced, transmitted, or stored in a retrieval system, in any form by any means, electronic, mechanical, photocopying, recording or otherwise, without the prior permission of the publisher.

The moral rights of the author have been asserted.

This is a work of fiction. Names, characters, businesses, places, events, locales, and incidents are either the products of the author's imagination or used in a fictitious manner. Any resemblance to actual persons, living or dead, or actual events is purely coincidental.

This book is sold subject to the condition that it shall not by way of trade or otherwise, be lent, resold, hired out or otherwise circulated, without the publisher's prior consent, in any form of binding or cover other than that in which it is published.

www.ukiyoto.com

Dedication

Dedicated to my wife late Mitali Bhuyan, who lead a beautiful life and tried to make world a beautiful, refined place for all through her continuous efforts.

Contents

What civilization is not?	1
Mature democracy is Civilization	2
Republic is not civilization itself	3
Indus valley civilization	4
We need new concept of Civilization	5
Be a civilization soldier	6
West need not teach civilization to others	7
Old civilization were also strong	8
Civilization will move further	9
Let us save our civilization	10
When we reach peak	11
Science and religion	12
Science and Technology	13
Are we supreme	14
Let's burry racial discrimination	15
Let us have a people centric society	16
I want a new world	17
Better tommorrow	18
Migration	19
No solution	20
Calamity	21
The world is on reverse gear	22
Past, present and future	23

Fundamental things are not man-made	24
Life	25
War is not solution	26
Be rational	27
Hongkong needs freedom	28
Suppression of Hongkong is wrong	29
Moral support	30
Primary Teacher	31
Thank you, Teacher on Teaher's Day	32
Good students respect teachers	34
Saffron	35
Free meal is bad economics	36
The idiot box	37
Weakness	38
Recognise others good qualities	39
Forgive leg puller	40
Love and sex	41
Is age just a number?	42
Accept your mistake	43
Covid19 is without cure	44
Decay	45
God can't see our misery and pain	46
Mind need exercise	47
Hesitation	48
In the greed for money and power	49
Time is not reliable now	50

I may not see your smile again	51
The beautiful poem	52
Clock is not time	53
Caste system is another form of racism	54
God Man	55
My lol	56
Society likes uniform conduct	57
I am not feeling good	58
If you are influential	59
Builders of Nation	60
Don't try to see problems everywhere	61
Take it easy	62
We are here for a limited period	63
Never doubt your will	64
Radiator	65
Don't cry	66
When I fall down from horse	67
Satisfaction	68
Patience	69
Eat, drink and sleep	70
Ozone Day	71
Don't keep your poetry pending	72
Check	73
Carelessness	74
Wife appreciation day	75
During old age, without wife you are zero	76

Criticising wife is dangerous	77
Grass on the other side	78
Different game	79
Survival of the fittest	80
Live in happiness, not in worry	81
The game is still on	82
Be a moon in my life, not star	83
Rose	84
To my heart rose is close	85
O' beautiful rose bud	86
Be careful	87
Emotional torture	88
Your fortune may not be readymade	89
I am mad for you	90
Don't hide behind your mask	91
Someone meeting God is imaginary	92
Faith	93
Couple challenge	94
Planning	95
Good immunity, better recovery	96
Greed for money	97
The nature is not fair	98
Religion is a dividing force	99
Emotions are like waves	100
O' my sweet darling	101
Integrity is great quality	102

Team will not appreciate negligence	103
Daughter is crown in our life	104
Optimism	105
Tourism is not merely sightseeing	106
Destination Northeast	107
Come and visit Shillong in Northeast	108
Arunachal, the land of rising sun	109
Come to Hornbill Festival of Nagaland	110
Save Assam's Pride	111
Kaziranga's Crown	112
Every time you may not be right	113
Winning is not, be all and end all	114
Dreams are strange part of life	115
Whom to blame?	116
Give and take	117
Give and take is like third law of motion	118
Give and take part of the game	119
Permutation-combination	120
Dream big	121
I am nothing	122
If you can't travel to the moon	123
Superiority complex breeds ego	125
Inferiority complex push to jealousy	126
Soul	127
IK IK Syndrome	128
Praise	129

Impartiality	130
If you are a gay	131
Lesbianism	132
Control your mind	133
Choose good companion for success	134
Avoid negative people	135
You will not live here forever	136
In the midnight	137
Root cause of India's problems	138
To weak, nature don't care	139
The road ahead	140
Let's cheer	141
For our loss no one will regret	142
World mental health day	143
Still scope to make life better	144
Our lifestyle has changed	145
Be bold to withstand pressure	146
Part of humanity	147
Departure of friend is painful	148
Take care of old friendship today	149
Friends can make life comedy	150
Better half	151
We must give resistance	152
International Day of Rural Women	153
Empathy	154
Kati Bihu, an Assamese Festival	155

Apple polish	156
Hesitation pushes to limitation	157
Don't worry about result	158
Make someone happy today	159
Think reality	160
Red rose	161
Extramarital love gives pain	162
We start life with a time bomb	163
Beggar has no choice	164
Blessings of beggars	165
Smile and smile	166
When the mind is quiet	167
To achieve goals be truthful	168
Broiler chicken	169
I am a powerful being	170
For survival time tested theme	171
When she said no	172
Cloud without rain	173
Action is better than reaction	174
I am a rolling stone	175
Pressure made me diamond	176
Free meal	177
Better remain shy	178
Cry for a while	179
Hiking	180
All wives are same	181

I can move alone	182
Love	183
Enjoy your money	184
Why world is round?	185
Man animal conflict	186
Be like quark	187
Think logically	188
Tik tok	189
O' my sweetheart darling	190
I am defeated by destiny	191
I love my country	192
Die with friendship	193
Gandhi	194
I like simple people	195
O God, lift your veil	196
Alcohol	197
Move on move on	198
Sankardev	199
I blame none for failure	200
Never tell a lie	201
Continue your journey	202
Knowing is not enough	203
Namghar (Assamese prayer house)	204
Namghosa (নামঘোষা)	205
Shankardev the unifier	206
Never stop momentum	207

Logic and wisdom	208
Don't sacrifice the innocent for God	209
Trust	210
Loneliness	211
Tentative existence	212
Save sea from pollution	213
When heart beats increase	214
Listen to your heart	215
Love is reciprocal	216
Midnight Sun	217
Mba	218
Degree	219
Religion	220
Diwali	221
Why we wakeup	222
Corruption in India	223
False promise	224
O' Lord, Open your eyes	225
We are moving towards hunger	226
UN is now silent spectator	227
Uncertainty Principle	228
Quantum entanglement	229
Genetic code	230
We are paranormal	231
Discrimination a global phenomenon	232
By-product of discrimination	233

Rapists need encounter of third kind	234
Abortion of female foetus	235
Male chauvinism is age old	236
Rape	237
Technology for better tomorrow	238
Work life balance	239
Need and greed	240
Population	241
About the Author	*242*

What civilization is not?

Hunting is not civilization,
Agriculture is civilization,
Fire is not civilization,
Cooking food is civilization,
Wheel itself is not civilization,
Cart and vehicle are civilization,
Coal is not civilization,
Steam engine is civilization,
Counting machine is not civilization,
Money and banking are civilization,
Printing machine is not civilization,
Spreading of knowledge is civilization,
Internet itself is not civilization,
ICT is civilization,
War is not civilization,
Peaceful living is civilization,
Civilization means improving quality of life,
For a better new world mankind must strive.
(ICT: Information Communication Technology)

Mature democracy is Civilization

When you can stand in the crowd without fear

You can express your voice without resistance and clear,

For disagreement, your paper no one will snatch and tear,

When people opposing you will not harm when you are near

Remember that the democracy is mature and dear,

Civilization is not winning country through power of gun,

It is not enforcing your thoughts, when people are on run,

Civilization is like the rainbow from the beautiful sun,

Every individual must be allowed to have his own life and fun,

Civilization is not shaping all individuals to same type of bun.

Republic is not civilization itself

Republic itself is not civilized democracy,

For this, we need people's competency,

Otherwise, democracy is word for fancy,

With empowered people, ruler has consistency,

The government will work as a serving agency,

There are republics ruled by dictator for religions and solvency,

In the name of religion, democracy remains in pendency,

To suppress democratic rights religious rulers' tendency

To suppress freedom of speech, they show arrogancy,

They kill people ruthlessly in the name of militancy.

Indus valley civilization

Three thousand years before Christ was born,

The Indus valley civilization has grown,

When people in many parts of world were nomadic

The urbanisation of Indus valley was scientific,

Existence of Mohenjo-Daro and Harappa is historic,

When the world was still in the clutches of darkness

Copper coin of Indus valley glow in brightness

The script of Indus valley is still mystery and undeciphered,

For drainage systems the people of the valley bothered

As one of the earliest civilizations, Indus valley is remembered.

We need new concept of Civilization

For centuries the prophets failed to bring peace in world

Like hot cakes only the religions and holy books were sold

Throughout the history of man, violence and wars unfold,

Misery of millions of people for religions remains untold,

For a better new world humanity should stand bold,

Tolerance levels of human beings should increase tenfold,

New concept of humanity and brotherhood remained in cold,

Value system for mankind all nations should uphold,

The stories of outdated prophets should remain unsold,

Time is ripe for new concept of humanity to take foothold.

Be a civilization soldier

Nature loves symmetry,
Nature also loves diversity,
It is our duty to maintain unity,
With nature make solidarity,
No two humans look similar,
But shape of every man is familiar,
Make unity within diversity popular,
Caste, creed, racism is destructive affair,
To all living things do good behaviour
Be a human values and ethics carrier,
God can't make our lives in earth easier,
For a better world everyone should be a soldier.

West need not teach civilization to others

West should not teach India civilization,
India never tried any colonialization,
Through Buddha, Indian did socialization,
Indian never tried monolithic polarization,
From India, the world learned toleration,
The west was not civilized during Indus valley time,
They were busy in hunting, robbery, and crime,
The European destroyed many good old democracy,
Second world war was because of their autocracy,
They tortured civilization a lot for supremacy.

Old civilization were also strong

Civilization is an irreversible process
Nature bear much pain and losses
Yet, nature provides us all resources
We refined and claimed as our successes
Many civilizations have gone to wilderness;
When we say our ancestors are uncivilized, we are wrong
During their times, their civilization was strong
Egyptian civilization also flourished and lived long
Our civilization will also decay and vanish
The beauty of modern life we should not tarnish.

Civilization will move further

Animal kingdom is surviving from viruses without any vaccine,

Nature must have given them some form of protective immune,

Without vaccines, man also crossed deserts with sand dune,

Viruses and animal kingdom all survived in the same commune,

Survival of the fittest is a time tested, time proven tune,

More viruses will mutate and come to the nature,

No one can predict and take precautions for future,

To reproduce rapidly in animal bodies, is viruses' culture,

Immunity of human body they always try to puncture,

Even with virus driven pandemic, human civilization moves further.

Let us save our civilization

God had not created any religion
Religion is human's imagination
God never told us to do pollution
To stop war, religion has no solution
Killing men for religion is men's creation;
Nowadays defunct all man made institution
God is hiding because of man-made destruction
Maybe for new incarnation, he is doing preparation
Or God maybe waiting for human's self destruction
It is duty of supreme animal to save its civilization.

When we reach peak

When civilization reaches peak
Its future becomes uncertain and bleak,
In this universe nothing is static
Everything is bound to be dynamic,
Time and change two sides of the magic,
From the peak no higher place to go
Spirit to move upward become low,
Nature will force civilization to decay,
Roses bloom only for few days stay,
Time and decay will move on its way.

Science and Religion

Civilization came through evolution
Science is part of forward solution
Mathematics doing precise calculation
Physics and math are in combination
Religion can never become substitution;
Life is beyond science and religion
None can give life's perfect definition
Too many differences in religious description
Science is also infant, and contradiction
Every life has its own way of visualization.

Science and Technology

After fire, wheel, paper, and printing press

Computer, smartphone and net is pushing our progress

Spreading of knowledge is important for civilization

Nowadays, the new technologies give better solution

Destruction of cities is technologies aberration;

For new generation, civilization means technology

No one bothers to know about the progress chronology

To live with ease and minimum work is human psychology

Only machines and robots can support us to live comfortably

In the long run, for comfort and progress it is science and technology.

Are we supreme

Sometimes I doubt, are we really animal supreme

Our behaviours to other living beings always extreme

For cohabitation even with men, we don't have scheme

Let us remember, all living beings are earth's raceme

Don't think, human alone have rights to eat nature's creme;

We claim ourselves as supreme animal in the planet

But our lives in the world is also like fishes in fishnet

Life of majority of supreme animal is not beautiful sonnet

Supreme animal is helpless in front of viruses, in the planet

Integration of plants, animals, and man necessary like internet.

Let's burry racial discrimination

The momentum of racial discrimination is now slow
Yet may parts of the world, sometimes it glow
To the mankind, racial discrimination is a blow
Together we must stop this inhuman flow;
Seven colours are part of the beautiful rainbow
With colour discrimination, we can't have better tomorrow
How can we think of beautiful eye without black eyebrow
Discrimination has given us lot of pain and sorrow;
The reasons for racial discrimination are swallow
Minds of people with discrimination are narrow
The very concept of racial discrimination is hollow
We have to burry discrimination under earth far below.

Let us have a people centric society

Why can't we have a society, that is people centric,
Our run for acquiring materials will not be hectic,
Even religious leaders grab of wealth is iconic,
Value of honest and good people in society is tragic,
Doing money and religion inseparable is strategic,
Money and religions, elite classes exploitation tool
With these two elements, people easily become fool,
So, in society, honesty and integrity now can't rule,
Yet, there are few honest and good people standing alone,
But it is increasingly becoming difficult to spread their clone.

I want a new world

A world without country
A world without boundary
A world without religion
A world without pollution
A world without constitution
A world without subversion
A world without restriction
A world without frustration
O' Lord give us a new world,
A new civilization we want to unfold.

Better Tommorrow

Every evening I hope for a better tomorrow
Always forget today's pain and sorrow
With the morning comes two sparrow
Happy that from the sun no need to borrow;
Today is a beautiful day with sunshine
For seeing two sparrow the day will be fine
To achieve higher, I forget to rest and dine
I can't waste to day because it is mine;
The silvery moonlight brings the reward
Even in the darkest night I move forward
I know tomorrow will come again with hope
So the darkness of night I can easily cope.

Migration

History of human civilization is migration
It can't be changed checking immigration
Through centuries people migrate for food
For survival of mankind, migration is good
Migrants can change productivity mood;
Once there was no nation and boundary
To protect resources man made country
Now, many people have to remain hungry
Passport, visa failed to stop movement
One world needed for civilization's improvement.

No solution

From time immemorial killing is the rule
Killing dissenting people considered cool
Killing to save our boundary is not crime
Killing people in enemy territory is prime
Killing is always fair during war time;
Killing is justified in Ramayana, Mahabharata
Killing in Karbala is the essence of Muhammad
Sometimes for religion, sometimes for nation
To kill people always open man's killing option
To prevent man killing man has no solution.

Calamity

We are stuck in manmade calamity
We have to overcome it with solidarity
This is testing time of our integrity
To overcome calamity is now priority
This is time to work for the humanity;
Blaming someone is not the solution
Let's try all permutation and combination
All research now needs integration
Working together will give better resolution
World must work with true determination;
The calamity has already sustained too long
If we don't stop it, day by day it will become strong
Delay to defeat it will be dangerous and wrong
The virus has already started to affect the young
Hope, soon mankind will sing together victory song.

The world is on reverse gear

The world is now on reverse gear
Environmental degradation is clear
Biodiversity is no more our dear
For deduction no one now fear
People only shed crocodile tear
Devastation is approaching near
Sound of melting pole we can hear
Species of animals extinct every year
One day we will face tragedy like King Lear.

Past, present and future

Future is resultant of past and present
Without present future is absent
Past can give only expert comment
In work of present future is latent
For better future present work important;
Summation of past and present is life
Future is only hope to become delight
Dream for future make present right
Build your present, past and future will be bright.

Fundamental things are not man- made

Man has not created day and night
Nor man made darkness and light
Man has not created life and death
Nor man has created natural wealth
Fundamentals are not our underneath;
Elements and atoms are not man-made
In nature fundamental things never fade
All natural things are of different grade
In cloning, natural things, man only remade
Day and night, life and death we can't trade.

Life

A beautiful, refined place for body and mind
For every living thing, life may not be kind
But in the morning for all a new day it unwind
Where pain or pleasure of life we have to find
With life comes, our death warrant duly signed;
Life is soft, fragile, uncertain but it is beautiful
So, make your life always better and cheerful
To others or your own life do nothing harmful
In world to make life happy, resources are plentiful
Smile and move on, life will become wonderful.

War is not solution

Time is relative
So it is sensitive
Fifteen become heavier
Forty is lighter
Peace is always brighter
Buddha was never hostile
Because love is very fragile
War is never a solution
Ashoka took peace resolution
Nuclear weapon should go hibernation
Let world work for terrorism dilution.

Be Rational

Corona should make man rational

In the name of religion don't be emotional

God, Allah no one come forward for rescue

We are fighting for them which is undue

Allah, God are business for selective few;

Pray to your god for your mental satisfaction

No quarrel please for the religious diversification

Christian, Muslim, Hindu no God came to save

To wage war for non-helping father no need to be brave

Through harmony for mankind better tomorrow we have to pave.

Hongkong needs freedom

From China, Hongkong needs freedom
Giving independence will be wisdom
China should not think agitation is random
Forever Hongkong will not be their fiefdom
Soon Hongkong will get joy of life seldom;
World community should work together
Let Hongkong become a nation forever
Trade and business will flourish again
The world community will immensely gain
The Chinese virus will break its chain.

Suppression of Hongkong is wrong

Let's work for freedom of Hongkong
People of Hongkong waited for long
We have to make movement strong
To support fight become one among
Suppression of Hongkong is wrong;
China is torturing innocent people
The demand of Hongkong is simple
Spirit of people China is trying to cripple
Support for Hongkong let's make triple
China must be forced to become humble.

Moral Support

Moral support in distress is value less
It will never help to overcome the mess
Moral support never removes financial stress
Rather for a penny you should press
Better help if someone gives a dress;
Moral support is like crocodile tears
It will not support to reduce your fears
You, yourself have to change your gears
Moral supporters are selfish coward
In their problems do give any reward.

Primary Teacher

O' thy worshipful soul
You made me whole
In my life you have role
Today I may be very tall
But on your feet, I will fall;
When I was too small
You responded my call
Even you played ball
Pulled me when I fall
For me you are above all.

Thank you, Teacher on Teaher's Day

In the journey of life
Some teachers we remember
They remain in heart forever
We forgot many things they taught
But we carry good teachers thought;
Good teacher is like an angel
The angel who was kind to Cinderella
He/she can change our life for better
In life we can think to achieve higher
We never forget him even after retire;
An ideal teacher is impartial to pupil
He is not rude but always compatible
In class he creates laugh and ripple
Every question he can easily dribble
Red card rarely uses even students' trouble;
A good teacher not only teach
But what he says, always preach

He is friendly and easy to reach
A selfless friend in the time of need
Make us good human through his deed.

Good students respect teachers

Respect to teachers is sign of good student

With good will teachers' compliment

In problem, teachers will always supplement

Teachers dislike cheating in the examination

They encourage students to give his own solution;

With father, mother, sister, friends and brother

The home teacher also become extended family member

Sometimes the role of good teacher is greater

Those who don't respect teachers will see failure

With respect to teachers and study, success is sure.

Saffron

The colour of courage and confidence
Symbol for not to take failure as precedence
Saffron colour is bright and beautiful all the time
Wearing saffron dress is not at all a crime
In Hinduism saffron colour is always prime;
Saffron colour keeps our mind cheerful
To any danger we don't become fearful
The colour gives peace even if situation is tearful
So, saffron is at the top of India's National flag
Nonviolence and brotherhood are also in saffron bag.

Free meal is bad economics

When government give free food
For economy it is not at all good
It changes people's working mood
On their foot no poor will stood
If not given free, they will be rude;
Sometimes subsidy is necessary
But in the long run it is reactionary
Empowerment of poor is more important
Forever free meal is economic deterrent
Interest free working capital is sufficient.

The Idiot Box

The idiot box is trying to be intelligent
But activities are same foolish diligent
Talk shows proves the box is really idiot
Trying to make people fool is the box's pivot
Always biased and motivated the box's report;
Entertainment is becoming day by day low
Though the box is maintaining its flow
Because of falsehood idiot box losing glow
For the box, social media is now a big blow
Because of own fault the box is now hollow.

Weakness

Don't think you are weak
If you think so, future is bleak
Everyone will try to kick
All your energy will leak
You will never reach peak;
Weakness is death
You die without wealth
Miserable will be health
Boldness is better life
Courage will strive.

Recognise others good qualities

Recognise good qualities in others
Appreciate them like your own brothers
But don't hide bad qualities like mothers
Mention them like responsible fathers
In their success you will find pleasures;
Don't measure everyone with same yardstick
All women never like the same colour lipstick
Every house is not made of the same brick
Everyone in life will not climb the same peak
Recognising people as they are is a helpful trick.

Forgive leg puller

When someone pulled my leg
I always put on him a mercy tag
Never I carry the revenge bag
When someone stab me on my back
I forgive him and ask to pack;
Leg puller taught you to be cautious
But back stabbers are very dangerous
The mindset of bac stabber is spurious
So, to back stabber be serious
Never allow them within your radius.

Love and Sex

Love without sex is pure
For mother's love be sure
When love end in sex
In the long run it is vex
It will burn like candle wax;
Sex without love is prostitution
It is only momentary physical solution
Sex with love is better combination
So, sex is also known as love making
Through love and sex exists human being.

Is age just a number?

People say age is just a number
But after sixty you are bad climber
In cricket no one wish them as runner
People always prefer young drummer
Though aged are better in grammar;
Mental age always remains young
But body of young people are strong
Experience of old people are long
So, they can avoid doing wrong
Youngster can sing better song;
Age has two sides, mental and physical
When both are in peak, people are practical
Nascent oxygen can do action miracle
But when stored it becomes simple
The physical side of life age always cripple.

Accept your mistake

China is not accepting their mistake
Rather, they are trying to dictate
The world economy is in quandary
China is diverting focus for boundary
For their mistake lot of people are hungry;
We have made a mistake, China should accept
For their falsehood, one day they will regret
Now nowhere in world China will get red carpet
From China many companies are buying return ticket
A small mistake of China emptied their own bucket.

Covid19 is without cure

The air was already impure
Corona now made it sure
Till now Covid19 has no cure
Contamination masks can secure
Vaccine no one can assure;
Pollution now becomes secondary
To save life from Corona is primary
School, college everything tertiary
Fear and uncertainty everywhere visible
Economy, Corona has come to cripple.

Decay

Everything in the world decay
I am constant no one can say
Decay and time move in tandem
Nature destroys things in random
Future is not in decay's fiefdom;
With decaying the bold become old
Free from decay not even pure gold
The beautiful youth no one can hold
To slow down decay, aging creams are sold
But only with decay life in world unfold.

God can't see our misery and pain

Allah is dumb, deaf and blind
Our misery and pain he can't find
So, most of the time he is unkind
Through prayer, we have to remind
Though God is capable to read mind;
We have to use loudspeaker for him
Light candles for heat and light beam
Yet God's voice no one has heard
Declaring as prophet some become smart
They say to our prayers God is always alert.

Mind need exercise

Mind also need healthy food
For us exercise of mind is good
Positive thoughts are good for mind
Through it, creative thinking you can find
For mind, good books are always kind;
Cleaning of mind is also necessary
Throwing hate and jealousy is primary
Greed is a dirty stain difficult to remove
But looking to to poor, you can dissolve
All our problems, healthy mind can solve.

Hesitation

Never perform jobs with hesitation
It will create unnecessary confusion
Vulnerable will be your own position
Always work with will and determination
For every problem you will find solution;
Hesitation slow down our day to day progress
In the long run we can't achieve our goals and success
Hesitation is always detrimental in business
With hesitation we fail to maintain persistence
Towards success, hesitation gives big resistance.

In the greed for money and power

In the greed for money and power
Own integrity people lower
Demolish his honest tower
Become falsehood whistle blower
But can't avoid fall down however;
When power failed to give happiness
They cry alone in pain and distress
Power can't bring back honesty back
Forever their integrity people will pack
Even with money, difficult will be life's track.

Time is not reliable now

Time is not at all reliable now
I am alive today, thank you God
Tomorrow will come as usual
But I may not be here to see it
Uncertainty is now at the peak;
Today is mine, because I am fine
So, I will sing, dance and dine
Though I can't invite you for wine
I pray, tomorrow also you shine
This year very good is growth of vine;
We may not meet again to hug
Time may pull from our feet the rug
My grave someone might have dug
Don't forget to call me in the evening
No guarantee, I will call you next morning.

I may not see your smile again

I don't know, I will see your smile again
All throughout the night there is heavy rain
Maintaining distance is now lifeguard main
To avoid meeting each other please train
Any moment we may fall in the deadly drain;
You are in my next door; I feel as usual
Though our meetings were very casual
I feel your presence through your smile
Under the mask now you may be hostile
I have lost my job and smile; it is now fragile.

The Beautiful Poem

The world is a beautiful poem
Sun is its controlling doyen;
Nothing in nature looks bad
Telling someone ugly is sad;
The river, hill, ocean all are poetry
Beautiful women are its Notary
For a better world poetry is votary
Poems are part of life without boundary;
The sky, moon, rain and the forest
For poetry all are always dearest;
The existence of poetry depends on world
Without nature poems will remain untold.

Clock is not time

The clock is not measure of time
Without clock also time run fine
My watch may be dead at night
But the sun rises at five AM right
Clock can't make my time bright
To make time right I have to fight
Time will give zeros if we take it light
Wasting time will make life full of plight
Life will become endless night.

Caste system is another form of racism

Symbol of caste people proudly show
Against caste system they never say no
So, the reform in India is very slow
But with reservation they dislike to go
To express superiority symbol has to bow;
Caste system is stumbling block to unity
For their own caste people show solidarity
In modern time caste system is liability
The orthodox rituals are only stupidity
A symbolic thread will not give superiority.

God Man

All God men are living devil
For society they are big evil
They are nasty fraud and thief
Their words never try to believe
Deceiving people, money they receive;
God men are ordinary notorious man
So, if you have sense, don't be their fan
Motive of God men is to earn easy money
In the name of God, they eat sweet honey
Educated people worshiping them is funny.

My lol

I miss you; I miss you
You are among selected few
Now I can't hug and kiss you
Regarding you, I have good view
But Corona is my beloved new;
For fear of Corona, I am avoiding all
My new beloved if strong and tall
To everyone I love you she call
In her love old and young all fall
I will not allow her to enter your hall;
Though Corona is very, very small
She can play all types of ball
Her hiding place can be even a doll
In abundance available in shopping mall
I am avoiding you to save from her my lol.

Society likes uniform conduct

Society likes to conduct uniform
If you differ, people say you are deform
Uniformity is law of the society
Nature always like diversity
If you think differently, they question integrity;
To think differently is your unique identity
You have the imagination to think differently
Today majority of people may not accept socially
But never give up thinking differently and logically.

I am not feeling good

I am feeling not good
Only job is eating food
To seniors God is rude
All of us are in bad mood;
Social gatherings Corona uproot
Lifestyle forced to reboot
No need to polish our boot
Outside home Corona can shoot
Very deep is now Corona's root.

If you are influential

If you are influential
Don't be judgmental
Keep your view confidential
People will say, it is political
Listen others also to be social;
Judgemental people are intolerant
They start quarrel at any moment
Don't realise, their view is not permanent
Listening others will always supplement
Respect those, who give views independent.

Builders of Nation

Engineers are builders of a nation
Without electricity no ration
No textile mills, no fashion
If water stops, lot of tension
Communication is now vision;
Fire, wheel, computer engineering invention
Engineer always gives us better solution
To do things better is engineers' resolution
Civilization moves on engineering and technology
Development of modern world is engineer's chronology.

Don't try to see problems everywhere

When you see problems everywhere
You can't move forward to anywhere
Instead looking for problems as excuse
Solve problems one by one and reduce
Accumulation of problems make it huge;
When you solve problem, you gain experience
With experience you can overcome all hindrance
Sometimes to solve problem you need persistence
Solving more and more problems will give you excellence
For success in life, you will easily overcome all resistance.

Take it easy

Take your tasks as easy
It will make you fully busy
Performance will be rosy
Life will always be cosy
You will never become drowsy;
Easy going attitude is best
Your approach no one can test
Tension will always be at rest
Enjoyment is maximum in fest
You can sleep well in your nest.

We are here for a limited period

We are here for a limited period
No one can tell how long he will live
So why accumulate, it is better to give
Don't spread hatred and violence
Sit alone and think being silent;
Join hearts with love and respect
In life you will find new prospect
Enjoy the joy of giving to others
You will feel all are your brothers
Years will no more be your life's measure.

Never doubt your will

Never doubt your will
Your dreams it will kill
With determination do drill
You can climb stiff hill
No need of any drug or pill;
If you doubt your capability
Your dream is impossibility
With fear don't show solidarity
Pursue your goals with sincerity
Success will be in your vicinity.

Radiator

Be a radiator of good thoughts
You will get good will lots
Good thoughts will not cost
But good thoughts we need most
Your good thoughts in Facebook post;
Be a radiator to cool the world
We are in global warming fold
The environment wants to be cold
So, we need radiator big and bold
Global warming, we must hold.

Don't Cry

When the dear one departs, don't cry
Better you should remain shy
Keep your both eyes dry
To give farewell with smile try
With heavy heart say goodbye;
He is going to meet the Father
So, sad situation is not better
Eternal peace the soul will get
This is the ultimate truth people bet
With flowers the last journey we set.

When I fall down from horse

When I fall down from horse
I run with him and maintain the course
Immediately I jump to his back
With both hands firmly hold his neck
Soon I am back in the racing track;
If you don't jump back immediately
Fear will engulf your mind slowly
Forever you may be from race
In racecourse no one will see your face
Getting up will be your winning base.

Satisfaction

Derive satisfaction in small thing
To your life happiness it will bring
Satisfaction don't lie in money alone
In your mind remain its clone
Through attitude it can easily born;
We get satisfaction if our team wins
Satisfaction comes wearing new jeans
In our children's success also, it rings
Friends companion may give satisfaction
We become satisfied when we reach destination.

Patience

Patience is a very important quality
Quick reaction is proven stupidity
With patience remain with solidarity
It will improve your social acceptability
Patience will also enhance personality;
Everything needs an incubation period
Impatience is a very harmful steroid
Even a banana needs time to ripe
The plumber needs time to rectify pipe
In life, your success, impatience can wipe.

Eat, drink and sleep

Our life is now like a pet dog
Can't go out because of virus fog
Lying on the bed for hours like log
Eat, drink and sleep without outing
In fear the whole world is burning;
We are afraid of welcoming people
Because he may infect to cripple
Suspicion is everywhere ample
For the virus is now not at all simple
Don't know how long we have to dribble.

Ozone Day

Saviour of life from ultraviolet rays
Without ozone limited will be our days
Ozone layer is important for life in earth
Without ozone shield radiation show warth
We must save ozone-oxygen cycles path;
For life, with oxygen, ozone is instrumental
Though quantity of ozone isn't substantial
Pollution has created holes in ozone layer
But to save the layer, few people are aware
The message of Ozone Day to everyone share.

Don't keep your poetry pending

Don't keep your poetry pending
Everything will vanish in the morning
Wake up in the midnight to note down
Next day your will lost your heart's sound
Once gone, the poetry is difficult to found;
Poems are emotional expression of mind
In every situation, moment you cannot find
To your inner voice always try to be kind
Immediately in your phone, the poem you bind
Afterwards for fine tuning any time you can rewind.

Check

Check your actions regularly
You can rectify fault surely
Check is necessary for rectification
Rectification will lead to perfection
Sometimes check gives required solution;
Regular check reduces chances of failure
It makes your actions better and secure
Check helps to do necessary change on time
To achieve the desired goal check on time is prime
Check of mind always helps from doing crime.

Carelessness

In your activity if you are careless
Your future will certainly be hopeless
Sometimes you have to be shameless
People will think you are baseless
Carelessness will make you restless;
When carelessness becomes habit
You can't come out of its gambit
You will lose the race even being a rabbit
Your carelessness tries to remove and edit
You will be successful in implementing your writ.

Wife Appreciation Day

Appreciate your beautiful wife
She is integral part of your life
Sometimes she may cut like knife
But without her indiscipline rife
So, enjoy with her day to day miff;
Wife is always friend in need
Though she may show greed
Nurture her like puppy of special breed
She will bear your next generation seed
Follow her, if a peaceful life you want to lead.

During old age, without wife you are zero

When you appreciate your wife
You appreciate your own life
After fifty, with wife you are hero
During old age, without wife you are zero
You friend circle will be limited and narrow;
Appreciate your bold and beautiful companion
In life she will make you all-rounder and champion
She will teach you how to balance life and work
Every moment she will deliver motivational talk
In the parties without beautiful wife how can you rock?

Criticising wife is dangerous

Criticising wife is very dangerous
It may push you to condition serious
You may have all the power and might
But always accept that wife is right
Otherwise, you position will be tight;
If wife criticise you, consider it for good
But if you criticise your wife, you will not get food
To you, ant moment wife may behave rude
But never try to upset her smiling mood
If she is angry, you may be forced to be nude.

Grass on the other side

Grass on the other side is always green
Neighbour's wife is always smart and thin
She always looks very, very beautiful
Always she smiles and remains cheerful
In small issues she never become tearful;
O' thy gentleman, peep to her house
From the bag, will come out the mouse
You will realise, how cool is your better half
In the locality most beautiful is your wife
With her you are lead leading good life.

Different game

The world is same
Different is game
Corona is the name
No use of fame
Without mask lame;
Who is to blame?
How it came?
China is the name
World must tame
Stopping Corona is aim.

Survival of the fittest

Survival of the fittest
E-books are now hottest
Cheaper in price
Smaller in size
To keep it nice;
Hard book is losing
E-book is amusing
For environment it is good
To nature hard book is rude
New generation has new mood;
Cloud has shadowed physical book
Though people like physical look
Technology is for better tomorrow
So, for physical book no sorrow
Without damage e-book you can borrow.

Live in happiness, not in worry

Live your life in happiness, not in worry
Worries will give you only pain and misery
Don't live with excuses and telling sorry
With love, write for life a fairy tale story
Till the end a smiling face you will carry;
Don't make life dumping ground of pain
To overcome hate and anger, yourself train
Throwing greed, beauty of living you will gain
Living with happiness should be resolution main
Give up worry, joy and smile will come in chain.

The game is still on

The game is still on
Don't stop, move on
The sun and moon on
The breeze is cool and on
Don't stop, move on, move on;
Life has still long way to go
So, don't make your speed slow
Trees are giving oxygen standing in row
Fight the enemy with crude arrow
But don't make your spirit low;
We may be in catch twenty-two situation
Move on to find a good solution
Promise that in future no more pollution
The journey is still on, so no hesitation
Move on, move on with determination;
Play the game together with team spirit
Together we will win make your instinct
Make humanity your value basic
Even for a moment don't become static
Momentum alone will give winning magic.

Be a moon in my life, not star

I don't want you to be a star in my life
You will be light years away, no light for me
Better you become a moon without light
Every full moon, I will see you being bright
For me seeing your beautiful face is right;
During darkness moon will give light to move
Like stars moon is not too far and too above
In the darkest night stars can never save
So, for me moon is always dear and I love
The stars are for me only symbolic dove.

Rose

Rose is the queen of flowers
Though its life is in hours
In garden it stands like towers
Beauty of its life always shares
When red rose rejected, comes tears;
For the thorn behind, no one fears
Beauty of rose everyone shares
Rose plant needs lot of cares
Bunch of roses is best gift to near and dears
Sadness of mind rose garden clears.

To my heart rose is close

My favourite flower is rose
To my heart it is very close
I love its fragrance dose
Loving spirit it can arouse
For photo, I can give best pose;
You can call rose by any name
Throughout the world it has fame
Rose's beauty nothing cam tame
It shines even in Corona flame
With rose, couple play give and take game.

O' beautiful rose bud

O' beautiful rose bud

Come out and smile

I am waiting for your fragrance

Will enjoy your beauty from distance

To our hard touch you have no resistance;

O' beautiful rose bud

Come out and dance in wind

In your colours we see the rainbow

Please open to us your window

Your thorns will protect you from hand's shadow.

Be careful

For whom you have bloom
Shining on shirt of groom
Your touch never makes gloom
You are welcome to every room
Rose are pride of every home;
In beauty and fragrance rose is best
Beauty of rose don't need supremacy test
Rose bloom to make world beautiful
In the garden, roses are always cheerful
To touch a rose, from thorn be careful.

Emotional torture

Emotional torture is dangerous
For revenge man become serious
It makes people ferocious
Sometimes it is like virus
Emotional torture is notorious;
Never do emotional torture
Some one's life it may rupture
It is not good for human culture
It may do your own life's puncture
Miserable will be your good future.

Your fortune may not be readymade

For everyone fortune is not readymade
To build a fortune you have to work decade
Your cutting edge should be like blade
Everyday sharpen your cutting edge
Even in night search for gold in salvage;
Luck gives fortune to very selected few
In business Gates, Ambani was once new
He knows how his food he should chew
Through persistence and work he grew
To make own fortune he had positive view.

I am mad for you

For you my heart is mad
So, I love you after rejection
You are in my heart is the satisfaction
I will not search for your location
Because you are my heart's companion;
My heart can never forget you
In my heart you are among selected few
Everyday your memory I will renew
For me you are evergreen and new
To love you, I don't need your cruel view.

Don't hide behind your mask

Simply don't hide behind your mask
In life, you may have pending task
Mask is only a small safety measure
Move ahead to find your life's treasure
How many masks you use is not life's measure;
If necessary, remove your mask to grow
For healthy life you need fresh oxygen flow
Don't allow masks to make your life slow
Masks can't give guarantee of the life
Mask is also like a double-edged knife.

Someone meeting God is imaginary

Someone meeting God is imaginary
But for blind people it is good story
So, the story spread beyond boundary
Clever people recast it in their foundry
For new story, blind people always hungry;
No prophet ever met the omnipotent
Omnipotent can never be inconsistent
To teach truth to all he is fully competent
But all prophet's teachings are different
So, prophets meeting God is fraudulent.

Faith

Faith is important for success
With positivity you can progress
Faith will also enhance courage
You can work with confidence
Fear will always remain in distance;
Without faith you can't feel the almighty
If you have faith, he will guide you rightly
Your life will glow with light brightly
Even in darkness you can move correctly
With faith success will come certainly.

Couple Challenge

Living together is the biggest challenge
You are successful, if you can manage
Every day couple faces new problems
Most of it remained in memory albums
If you can delete, you can do good programs;
Couples are three legged runners
Both must clean their home's burners
Mutual understanding is the rule of law
Both the runners may have different flaw
For couples, divorce is the death's jaw.

Planning

My planning calendar is now blank
For this whom should I thank
Now I am again in children rank
For money sometimes I visit my bank
I have to fill my body's stomach tank;
My movements are now restricted
So, planning can't be properly fabricated
All my future planning Covid19 humiliated
My future planning is now in hibernation
I will plan only after Corona vaccination.

Good immunity, better recovery

Don't be overconfident on mask
Hand wash can also do limited task
Vaccine may also have side effects
Sanitizer are supplied with defect
Against all, only immunity is perfect;
Nature has given us unique immunity
Exercise, good food needed for continuity
Medicine only supports healing process
It can't cure every patient who is in distress
With good immunity, better chance of success.

Greed for money

Greed for money is also a disease
Every day the thrust for it increase
More money means more reinvestment
For greedy people there is no retirement
For the earning money is only pertinent;
Greedy think, in world they are permanent
So, earning money is their only satisfaction
They think in life money is the solution
Greedy people are the most insecure
They depart from world with worry, be sure.

The nature is not fair

To the deer, nature is not fair
Always they have to live in fear
With tigers, the same jungle they share
But they get killed by tiger, if they go near
In jungle nobody is deer's friend and near;
The world is not fair, accept the reality
It will bring to mind peace and tranquillity
Struggle in the unfair world for survival
Soon you will see your successful revival
Survival of fittest is the rule universal.

Religion is a dividing force

Religion is a dividing force
India-Pakistan is historical source
Through division took different course
Religious divisions are very worse
It is worse than hunger and divorce;
Originally from same civilization
Religion made a permanent division
Both are fighting without solution
Though India is in a better position
Nuclear war will bring both countries destruction.

Emotions are like waves

All that glitters are not gold
Your poetry may remain untold
But in your heart always hold
They will make you brave and bold
Some emotions are not to be sold;
Emotions are like waves of ocean
It comes and goes very fast and often
But our hearts, every time it soften
All feelings impossible to be written
Its capture happens all of a sudden.

O' my sweet darling

I love you not because you are beautiful
I love you because you are always cheerful
I love you not because you are resourceful
I love you because you are not harmful
I also love you because you are beautiful;
I love you because you are always smiling
I love you because you are very caring
I love you because you know flirting
I love you because you are kind and sharing
I love you because you are my sweet darling.

Integrity is great quality

If your integrity is doubtful
Your life will become shameful
You will be considered as harmful
Your actions will be considered wilful
Your critics in society will be plentiful;
A precious and great quality is integrity
It is also other side of the coin honesty
Without integrity no one will trust you
You will be in the gang of criminals few
Once lost, integrity can't come back new.

Team will not appreciate negligence

Negligence can shatter your dream
It will not be appreciated by your team
In teamwork negligence is weakest beam
A small negligence can spoil pot of cream
Your future in the team will be grim;
Mistakes people are ready to forgive
But negligence is considered negative
Through checking take action corrective
Revision makes your performance effective
Avoid negligence for result to be positive.

Daughter is crown in our life

Crown in our life is a daughter
She is always very dear to father
Some one's daughter is our mother
Without her life can't flow further
Her smile every moment inspire;
Daughter is the best gift from heaven
Father's love to daughter never weaken
In the desert of life, she is a flowing spring
In the family, happiness she can bring
Even in hard days she can inspire to sing.

Optimism

In life for success, we must be optimistic
Without optimism life becomes static
Optimism inspires to move forward
In the struggle of life always expect reward
Pessimist people are generally coward;
Optimism gives us positive push to move
Life is full of opportunities it always prove
Optimistic people are happy and smiling
They know, tomorrow sun will rise again
Forever the darkness will never remain.

Tourism is not merely sightseeing

Tourism is not merely sightseeing
Change to life it can easily bring
Seeing is believing, mind's bell it rings
To fly, it opens your attitude and wings
Your approach to life becomes like kings;
Sightseeing alone is not called tourism
It infuses cultural diversity and pluralism
Tourism helps society to overcome racism
It is a thread for integration of humanism
Tourism always breeds cultural socialism.

Destination Northeast

Destination Northeast of India
Attention to all national media
The biodiversity hot spot welcome you
Your visit to the Rhino land is due
Visit Assam and enjoy Kaziranga's view;
A cruise on Brahmaputra is mind blowing
In your mind, forever it will be flowing
Picturesque is evergreen forests and hills
A journey by road in Northeast always thrills
With taste of ethnic food your stomach fills;
A trip to Northeast you will never regret
The hospitality of people heart will not forget
To visit Kamakhya and Majuli make your next target
Angling and rafting in Northeast is breath-taking
Monsoon clouds and waterfalls are captivating.

Come and visit Shillong in Northeast

Come and visit Shillong
You will find hills all along;
The place of cloud is Meghalaya
Its beauty is tall like Himalaya;
Scotland of India is verdant and wondrous
A visit to Shillong is always pleasures;
Cherapunji gets world's highest rainfall
To visit again and again it's beauty will call;
Shillong was once capital of Northeast
With lakes, waterfalls it is destination best.

Arunachal, the land of rising sun

The land of rising sun is Arunachal
In Northeast it is another Himachal
Tawang is famous for Buddhist heritage
To do rock climbing, you need courage
Visit to Madhuri lake is not time wastage;
Come to Arunachal during the orange festival
You will enjoy homemade wine in the carnival
People have to work hard for their survival
But the state is full of hydroelectric potential
Visit to Tawang, Bhalukpung, Mesuka will be memorable.

Come to Hornbill Festival of Nagaland

Come and enjoy hornbill festival
Promote the endangered bird's survival
The beauty of hornbill is classical
Hornbill festival promote Naga heritage
Original lifestyle modernity unable to sabotage;
Insurgency is no more irrelevant for the people
They are now willing to welcome being humble
The economy of the state now needs to jump triple
Tourism can bring new dimension and ripple
Come to Nagaland and enjoy its thick jungle.

Save Assam's Pride

Rhino is Assam's pride
Let's make their future bright
Eviction of encroaches is right
To save their habitat we must fight
Miracle of Rhino horn is only myth;
Poaching of Rhino is for superstition
Campaign is necessary for its solution
Awareness will make demand dilution
We are duty bound for Rhino preservation
Killing of Rhino is always Assam's humiliation.

Kaziranga's Crown

Kaziranga's Crown is Rhino
It is like a priceless piano
Grassland necessary of its food
For Rhino damp humid climate is good
Felling of trees in Kaziranga is really rude;
Moderate flood helps grass to grow
Without its lifeline of Kaziranga will not grow
Birds also needs wetlands for survival
Destruction of wetland is criminal
For the animals of Kaziranga be humble.

Every time you may not be right

Every time you may not be right
So, argue but don't start a fight
Don't try to show your might
Your position may become tight
It will be proved, you are light;
Accept the truth when you are wrong
It will prove, you are mentally strong
Your mind will always remain young
Truth sounds like a melodious song
With friends and foes, you can walk long.

Winning is not, be all and end all

In love and war everything is fair
So, runners up trophy are rare
Your win everyone will not share
Even your friends may not care
Win may become your nightmare;
Winning is not, be all and end all
It may also lead to your great fall
Move with fair play even if step is small
Everyone will listen to your call
In the long run you will stand tall.

Dreams are strange part of life

Dreams are strange part of life
During sleep it comes and swipe
Sometimes good, sometimes bad
Sometimes it pushes us to red
Sometimes dream make us mad;
Reflections of unconscious mind
Sometimes in dreams life we find
But horrifying dreams are unkind
In the morning when we try to rewind
Most of the time, can't be recalled by mind.

Whom to blame?

Brutality in blue films is shame
For it whom we should blame?
So called modern society promote it
Because for their pleasure it fit
On the head the nail needs hit;
Forced prostitution is as bad as rape
But it is a business in legalised shape
Sex slave and harem still exist in society
Without mindset change how to change polity?
Gender discrimination is a hard reality;
Trafficking of poor girls is day to day affair
Racketeering money many people share
For gender equality police never care
In gender discrimination rape is only one form
The mindset and attitude of society needs total reform.

Give and take

Give and take, give and take
Your progress you can make
Without giving you can't bake
Rationality, fair play is fake
Give, people will come to lake;
Give and take is law of nature
So, it is not a negative culture
Every action has opposite reaction
By giving, you can expect action
Give and take should be in rotation.

Give and take is like third law of motion

Every action has equal and opposite reaction

Habit of give and take always keep in motion

For survival in world, don't forget it till cremation

Without give and take some problems have no solution

In life give and take will help you to control tension;

When you give, you draw others attention

To be friendly, you will get quick permission

So, to the habitat of give and take show no hesitation

For success in life, give and take is a good combination

Without giving if you only take, you will lose the direction

Apply the trick of give and take in life with determination.

Give and take part of the game

Every rung in the ladder takes our weight
But to say thank you we always forget
If you don't give, one day you will regret
You will miss you path, goal and regret
Even to get love, you must care your pet;
In give and take there is no shame
It is part of our family life's game
In society without giving you are lame
You are foolish, if you try to tame
For your failure, you yourself to blame.

Permutation-Combination

When to pray God, we give him respect
In return something we always expect
At least our expectation is better prospect
Our give and take attitude we never distract
From our mindset give and take we can't subtract;
God also follow his universal laws of motion
Realising it, to temples people give good donation
By giving, they want to take own problem's solution
The universe exists only through universal gravitation
For success, give and take is the only permutation-combination.

Dream big

Always dream very big
To get gold we must did
It's not easy like wearing a wig
But it should not be like pig
No liquid gold without rig;
For success dreams are important
But planning is more significant
To make it real you must be prudent
Every small step is pertinent
Without work it dream will become silent.

I am nothing

In the universe, I am nothing
Every moment life is diminishing
Only for some time I am shining
With family and friends smiling
To welcome grave is silently waiting;
In the world we are like a soap bubble
To live longer always struggle
But in a moment, we may tumble
So, in life always be nice and humble
Even in a bubble, rainbow is visible.

If you can't travel to the moon

If you can't travel to the moon
Visit great wall in China soon
Look at the sky on full moon night
From moon also great wall is bright
Enjoy as if now you're on moon right;
If you can't swim across the Pacific Ocean
Swim across the channel in summer season
To show your capability this can be a reason
When you are angry, do show your emotion
Silence will always give you better solution;
If you can't climb a tall tree in the forest
Look to the birds from the homely resort
You will enjoy the singing of the parrot
During travel if you lose your passport
To the nearest police station quickly report;
If you can't drive a motor car of your choice
Higher a vehicle for the journey and rejoice

The food in a five-star hotel is also same
Eating on roadside don't think you're lame
For your unhappy thoughts, no one is to blame;
To enjoy life, always no need to have the best
When tired of work, any bed comfortable to rest
A hungry stomach doesn't bother for good taste
Thank God for the beautiful things he has given
Enjoy with it today, tomorrow is always uncertain.

Superiority complex breeds ego

Superiority complex breeds ego
To respect others feeling we forgo
Ego is always a down fall logo
Achievements will become long time ago
As if you lost road in jungles of Congo;
Ego and superiority complex destroy man
People quickly lost all well-wishers and fan
With ego no one can accept his mistake
To repeat it superiority complex will dictate
Soon you will be in the arrogance basket;
Never insult anyone as inferior creature
Everyone has unique purpose in nature
In life superiority complex is bad culture
Life's beautiful journey it can puncture
Superiority complex and ego spoils dossier.

Inferiority complex push to jealousy

Inferiority complexes make us jealous
In life jealousy is always hazardous
Jealousy can breed hate story dangerous
It will spoil your happiness precious
To stop inferiority complex be serious;
You are not inferior to anybody else
Comparisons can worse your case
Always strengthen your own base
With confidence, your goal you chase
Ignore with smile, if someone try to tease.

Soul

Body, mind, knowledge and wisdom
All together is the soul's kingdom
Without soul life has no real value
Where the soul exists, no one has clue
But respect every soul and give his due;
You can't separate soul from your life
Soul is always like an inseparable wife
No one can kill your soul with sharp knife
soul is our real identity immortal, infinite
Listen to your soul, life will fly like kite.

IK IK Syndrome

I know, I know is hindrance to learning
You will be busy only in money earning
Learning is a continuous process
Only learn and unlearn can give success
To know new things with others, discuss;
In learning IK IK syndrome is big hindrance
To be a good learner, one needs persistence
In acquiring knowledge, I know gives resistance
With IK IK syndrome failure is not a coincidence
To acquire knowledge, keep IK IK syndrome at distance.

If you are a gay

If you are a gay
For you night is day
Different is your way
You don't see nature's ray
Dislike to swim in the bay;
Nature made you unnatural
To your own gene you are cruel
You don't want to make it plural
Your gene can't go to your funeral
In society you are like the vowel.

Lesbianism

Lesbian's rights are now legally protected
From society they can't be legally ejected
In some societies they are still rejected
People insult them when they are detected
With same sex marriage society is infected;
Psychiatrists say lesbians not unnatural
There are some lesbians who play duel
But to lesbians many people are cruel
Many lesbians are successful jewel
Yet in the nature lesbianism not natural.

Control your mind

Control your fickle mind
Destination you will find
Uncontrolled mind is unkind
Any direction it flies with wind
Learn, how your mind you can bind;
Uncontrolled mind is speeding car
It can't travel safely very far
Any moment it can make accident
So, controlling though is important
Who can't control mind, are ignorant.

Choose good companion for success

If you wish to be a champion
Always choose good companion
Friends influence with their opinion
Bad companion will do goal distortion
With them, you will take wrong direction;
Good companion motivates to achieve goal
Through team spirit they inspire your soul
They will pull you whenever you fall
During sadness, they will certainly call
In success, friend's contribution is not small.

Avoid negative people

When you avoid negative people
Your life becomes easy and simple
Every move you need not dribble
You can avoid too many trouble
With negative though you don't cripple;
Avoid negative people for success
Every morning you will see progress
Your mind's garden will be full of roses
You will be determined to fulfil wishes
Soon you will be at top with new dresses.

You will not live here forever

Majority of people think they will not die
In the journey of life to everyone they lie
To amassing money, wealth they always try
In the world of greed, falsehood they fly
But when the end comes, they loudly cry;
Death is ultimate truth we must remember
We are not going to stay in world forever
Today's king, tomorrow may become beggar
So, your money and wealth for good cause share
In the last journey, people will give respect rare.

In the Midnight

In the darkest midnight
In the soft bed everything is right
Hard battle two souls' fight
To make their future bright
They become tired in morning light;
Nothing is indecent in the bed
The surrounding is already dead
With emotions faces become red
For future life, eggs should be laid
To fertilize male-female union is made.

Root cause of India's problems

Root cause is population explosion
With it we can't find any solution
Poverty will remain as India's humiliation
There will not be control of pollution
The nation needs childbirth restriction;
Flood, unemployment all is secondary
Population control in India is primary
Development will remain as tantalus cup
To become developed nation, we can't jump
For India population is cancerous lump.

To weak, nature don't care

The life in earth is not fair
So, our wealth we don't share
To weak, nature don't care
Survival of weakest is rare
No one listen distress prayer;
To survive we become selfish
Otherwise, any time we may perish
Everyday weaker species diminish
In hostile we have to fill our dish
No one wishes, his life should extinguish.

The Road Ahead

The road ahead is not to afraid Corona
The WHO protocol has lot of lacuna
The time is now to learn self defence
Herd immunity will fight the offence
Individual will give to virus own resistance;
All bans, restrictions should be lifted
To us, our old good days should be gifted
No new protocol should be drafted
New lockdown must be resisted
Fear psychosis from society to be evicted.

Let's Cheer

O' my friend dear
For Corona don't fear
Again, move on top gear
The road ahead is clear
No need to look rear;
The past doesn't need repair
Future is very near
Enjoy sweet pear
With friends' drink beer
Together let's cheer.

For our loss no one will regret

One day in future people will forget
For our loss no one will regret
They will have their own target
Costly will be their own budget
We are out through hit wicket;
Time has put barrier and picket
We all are bound to listen dictate
Whole humanity is now necked
Soon the time will change and rotate
But by that time empty will be our basket.

World mental health day

Mantel health is equally important
For life body and mind both pertinent
When body and mind you synchronise
In the morning confidently you can rise
When mental health is good, you are wise;
Celebrate world mental health day
To the mentally ill distribute hope and ray
Don't ignore depression of your mind
Discuss with doctor, solution you will find
To the mentally retreated always be kind.

Still scope to make life better

And life flows like this
Epidemic, pandemic
Flood, earthquake
Volcano and tsunami
But never stopped for a moment
Civilization move on with faster speed
Fire, wheel, electricity and computer
All the discoveries to make life better
The wars failed to stop the moment
Celeron, Pentium, dual processor
Moving in tandem with expanding universe
Every setback mankind faced with courage
Yet poverty is still throughout the globe
Hungry people are forced to move
Discrimination, racial or gender
Still roam in the society together
However, in the graveyard same cry
Reality is that one day everyone will die
By instinct life and death will flow forever
There is still scope to make world better.

Our lifestyle has changed

Happy at our lifestyle change
Husband-wife together we manage
We may be confined in two rooms cage
But wild geese we need not chase
Home is now our bonding base;
From mind, party times we erase
In life that was a different page
Beauty of those days now we can gauge
The time has forced us to a new phase
In the family life we are feeling amaze.

Be bold to withstand pressure

If you can withstand the pressure
You are capable to find treasure
Your efforts time will rightly measure
Success will give you enough pleasure
Beautiful life you will enjoy in leisure;
Pressure helps rice to boil quickly
The pressure of of work deal smartly
In life problems will always be in plenty
Play it like the cricket match of county
Never allow pressure to make mind dirty;
Pressure change coal into diamond
But diamond is not everywhere found
Coal has to withstand pressure around
Then only as diamond coal is crowned
Only on time, pressure cooker makes sound.

Part of Humanity

Religion, politics are part of humanity
Without mankind they don't have identity
With mankind they must go with solidarity
So, goal of religion, politics must be unity
Tolerance needed to accept the diversity;
Without human values world is animal kingdom
Survival of fittest will rule the earth's fiefdom
No need of society, law because of absolute freedom
Killing others for survival will be only wisdom
Requirement of religion, politics will be seldom.

Departure of friend is painful

Departure of a friend is always painful
The time we spend with him was joyful
To take our care good friends are careful
Best friends remain in heart and respectful
Forgetting the help of friends is sinful;
Friends will come and friends will go
Your hospitality to friend today please do
Tomorrow he may be busy and say no
Circumstance may made him your foe
To cruel death, without meeting he may bow.

Take care of old friendship today

Today take care of your friend
Tomorrow maybe you're the-end
A gratitude message today send
Put forward your helping hand
Meeting at graveyard is bad trend;
Small ego may make friends separate
After his departure no point in regret
The small difference today please forget
Smile with him and play friendly cricket
To join broken friendship today is target.

Friends can make life comedy

Not having good friend is tragedy
Only friends can make our life comedy
Friends support to hold when air is windy
During a journey, friends are always handy
Without friend life is desert like sandy;
Friend will give an umbrella on rainy day
In the dark night with torch will show ray
True friend will never ask your monthly pay
Will never put hindrance on your rosy way
Your good qualities to others they say.

Better Half

You are the wisest, kindest, most beautiful person
So, with love, I stand by you, during all the season
For me our beautiful, sweet home is not like a prison
Discussing with you, I find all my problems solution
Your love and affection are my successful life's reason;
Your smile is the inspiration in the darkest night
So, with confidence next morning I can fight
When you accompany me, my day become bright
You are my child's mother, the torch with light
O' my better half, I always accept you are right.

We must give resistance

The river has its usual flow
The sun has not lost its glow
But world economy become slow
The poor people got a big blow
Totally changed our daily show;
Uncertain our temporary existence
Yet we must give our resistance
With masks cover some more distance
For survival mankind need persistence
Civilization always faces tough hindrance.

International Day of Rural Women

They work hard to feed their children
Yet their contribution remains hidden
Rural women carry maximum burden
But bloom as flowers of forest garden
Due to poor healthcare, death is sudden;
For family they sacrifice everything
After feeding children, remain nothing
With smile starts next day's counting
Quietly ignore husband's shouting
Every morning they start survival fighting;
Move to paddy field after household work
For road construction break hard rock
But their education the rural society lock
During old age their boats hit the dock
Totally deprived is rural women flock.
(15 October is International Day for Rural Women)

Empathy

Always don't try to show your sympathy
For better understanding we need empathy
When we see the situation with others eye
To our judgemental approach we say bye
To feel the pain through others heart, try;
Sympathy is skin deep, empathy is deeper
When you listen with own ears, voice is clear
The batsman only knew how difficult was the ball
But from galleries it is easy to give experts call
In comparison to sympathy, empathy is very tall.

Kati Bihu, an Assamese Festival

During flood, people struggle for survival

The water gives inspiration for revival

The green paddy fields make people jovial

The festival of Kati Bihu is always social

Eating of citrus fruits in field is historical;

People pray to God for safety of cultivation

If crop is damaged, they will be in starvation

Flood had already done too much of devastation

The sky lamp in the field will welcome a better tomorrow

Looking at golden rice, people will forget their sorrow.

(Kati Bihu is an Assamese Festival celebrated when paddy fields

 become dark green in the month of October. It is a festival of GREENERY)

Apple polish

If you do apple polish
You can avoid anguish
Your bad points will vanish
With promotion you will flourish
Without apple polish, you will perish;
Apple polish is golden rule of promotion
Only with good work never expect elevation
One mistake will all good jobs dilution
No one will give value to your emotion
In apple polish don't do any hesitation.

Hesitation pushes to limitation

Don't make your companion hesitation
In every walk of life, you will see limitation
To face challenges, you will lose determination
For fear of defeat you will quickly go to hibernation
Instead of success, you will face humiliation;
Hesitation is hindrance for forward movement
With courage and confidence face every situation
Don't allow hesitation to make your mind's pollution
Without hesitation work for the best solution.

Don't worry about result

Give attention to your work
Don't think about the result
The result is in uncertain future
Before starting, if you think about puncture
You will be afraid to move further;
Plant the tree without thinking about fruit
First try to strengthen its root
One day some kids will come with boot
By that time, you may not be there
But the tasty fruits they will remember;
Performing the job with satisfaction is best
After completion, with smile take rest
Bother for your report card least
The result is in others hand to test
Enjoy your evening with friends and guest.

Make someone happy today

Make someone happy today
Don't wait for his birthday
You may be sick on that day
No need to wait till weekend
Keep it free for your girlfriend;
Today is the best time to make someone happy
Tomorrow the journey may be tough and bumpy
When you see happiness in others face
For your happy tomorrow it builds base

Think Reality

Think only of things you want in reality
Work with planning to make it certainty
Reality is always continuous discontinuity
It is also a discontinuous continuity
To achieve reality, you need integrity;
Don't think imaginary things, you can't make
Your life and peace of mind it will break
When you dream, you must make it real
Otherwise whole life, defeated you will feel
Make your dream real with determination and zeal.

Red Rose

Red roses are really awesome
Among flowers they are handsome
The colour is beautiful and bright
For signals also the red colour is right
But in football red is tight;
Red rose garden is mind blowing
The beauty and fragrance are ever flowing
The gift of red rose is always exciting
Beautiful wall hanging is red rose painting
To present girlfriend red rose is fascinating.

Extramarital love gives pain

Wherever you go, my shadow will follow
Even a single moment you can't forget
My absence every moment you will regret
To unite with me will be your only target
You will never try to fill your empty pocket;
I loved you from my heart with sincerity
Never I doubted your love and integrity
In every walk of life, I accompanied with honesty
But you are attracted by by extramarital love
Now whole life with regret and alone you move.

We start life with a time bomb

We all start our journey in the womb
But we start life with a time bomb
No one knows when the bomb will explode
Only time and destiny know the code
With billion dollars, explosion you can't hold;
Sometimes it explodes too early in childhood
To family and friends, the shock becomes rude
Sometimes it explodes too late but gives lot of pain
But uncertainty over explosion time always remain
The final journey even best doctors can't retain.

Beggar has no choice

Beggar has no choice
They speak in low voice
No one beg for fun
To meet hunger, some take gun
Snatching money some people run;
But some are professional beggar
For society they create danger
They are not happy meeting hunger
Sometimes they become burglar
Begging as profession is easier.

Blessings of Beggars

Blessings of beggars is like fair and lovely
The blessings never work on people timely
So, it is better to ignore those wisely
Blessings had never worked for me properly
Otherwise, I would have become billionaire surely;
Fair and lovely has not made all users fair enough
Even with so much of blessings my life is very tough
Had blessings worked properly, I will be Bill
I could have found software, viruses to kill
With so many blessings, life's journey is stiff hill.

Smile and Smile

Even under the mask smile and smile
Though the present situation is fragile
If you stop smiling, it can become habit
So, from your smiling face don't debit
Even if no one can see, always repeat;
Flowers are smiling in garden as usual
The animal and butterfly are still casual
Soon masks will become past ritual
We will again become animal social
Carry on practice of smiling as trial.

When the mind is quiet

When the mind is quiet
Bad thought can't bite
You can think right
The divine show the light
You can overcome your plight;
Quiet mind finds new idea
But don't disclose it to media
Media will make idea's dilution
Incubate your innovation
You will find patentable solution.

To achieve goals be truthful

To achieve goals, be humble and truthful
Though the journey may be very painful
Even if you fail, you will not become sinful
Your approach to reach goal not wilful
To your soul, you will not be shameful;
To achieve goal, be trustworthy and dutiful
But to anyone never ever become harmful
To achieve goals, opportunities are plentiful
So, with people and situations be playful
Even if you can't win, the game will be beautiful.

Broiler Chicken

God created man and woman and ordered to multiply
To feed man now, broiler chicken God supply
Cruelty to animals, to broiler chicken doesn't apply
Survival of the fittest will also be God's easy reply
Without broiler chicken, meat will be in short-supply;
For man, broiler chicken is not a living creature
So, broiler chicken can withstand any torture
Broiler chicken born and die without any future
When gained weight, man send them to butcher
God also wishes broiler chicken should not live longer.

I am a powerful being

I am a powerful being
I will achieve great thing
I have heard God's ring
To fly, I will open my wing
The trophy, I will bring;
I am powerful, so I am cool
I will follow the path of rule
I am magnetic to attract trust
All my opponents will bite dust
I am determined, my win is must.

For survival time tested theme

Give and take is religious teaching
People say it has God's blessing
Everyone benefited from harnessing
It has developed from the barter system
For survival, it is time tested theme;
You pay to buy daughter's favourite doll
The joy you see on her face is not small
All relationships strengthen on this call
Without gift you can't celebrate X-mas well
Santa also comes will gift ringing his bell.

When she said no

When she said you no
Take your way and go
Never try to tow
Otherwise, she will become foe
Don't make self-esteem low;
When she said no, it is final
She will not go for any trial
The news soon will be viral
Your actions will be anti-social
Hundred number she will dial;
When she said no, don't send gift
It will widen mistrust and rift
Better your location you shift
To you slowly she may drift
Don't take action too swift;
When she said no, don't look back
To move out, quickly do your pack
Clean your relationship rack
Her Facebook don't try to hack
On your birthday she will bring cake.

Cloud without rain

Your knowledge and skills may be priceless
If you don't utilise it for mankind, it is useless
People will believe your claims are baseless
To utilise your knowledge effectively be restless
Without use, your cooking skill is forever tasteless;
Don't allow your knowledge and skills to rust
To sharpen it, frequent utilisation is must
Otherwise at the hour of need, your skill you can't trust
When you distribute knowledge, you equally gain
Knowledge not distributed is cloud without rain.

Action is better than reaction

Action is always superior than reaction
Only action can determine your direction
Reaction comes with too many reservation
Action is for a result or to find solution
Reaction comes to change the situation;
In life it is necessary to be active, not reactive
Reactive actions can never become distinctive
If you think too much about reaction, you can't act
For your failure in life, this is also a true fact
Act now and deal with all reactions with tact.

I am a rolling stone

In the friction of time
I am a rolling stone
Time has made me plain
The friction removed all stain
Sometimes on hilly spring
Sometimes on the river bed
Time flow above me
The truck carries to sunny road
Bearing severe pressure and pain
I wait for good days and rain
But my hope goes in vane
Only sorrow and tears I gain
In the long run my surface become smooth
The morning rays reflect rainbow
The butterfly rests on my surface
The child said "wow what a beautiful stone!"

Pressure made me diamond

The pressure of pain made me strong
I survived millions of years long
Though I was carbon abandoned
Time changed me to become diamond;
Persistence and perseverance make you bold
A brave new world everyday unfold
New history is made which was untold
At premium your innovation will be sold;
Whenever you fall down in the journey
Immediately stand up and start the tourney
While fetching honey the bee may bite
But for the best taste you must fight;
The pleasure and pain two sides of the coin
You will be successful if both side you can join
Difficulties and hurdles are only dotted line
Attitude and hard work make everything fine.

Free meal

In the world no free meal
But your money can be steal
People will come with fake deal
Every moment they will try to kill
No one will come forward to heal
In the sea will sink your zeal
Forever your future will seal
Your bank balance will be nil
You will be unable to pay bill
No money even to buy pill
Never run after free money and meal
Work hard with determination and will.

Better remain shy

Never hurt anybody's soul
You will score only self-goal
Harsh words are like boomerang
Never allow it to come to tongue
Word once told can't be taken back
In future it may again reflect and rack
Word is omnipotent never it die
Always speak the truth not a lie
Your foul word may force a friend to cry
When angry better to remain shy.

Cry for a while

When heart is full of sorrow
Rain is needed for better tomorrow
Crying is not always a bad thing
Lot of relief to mind it can bring
The tears will wash away pain
Clear will be your chocked drain
Smile will come back to your face again
For the heart crying is like rain
Don't allow negative emotions to pile
Bring rainbow to life crying for a while.

Hiking

Hiking is always better than biking
Satisfactory is also bicycle riding;
Walking on countryside is good
It can enlighten and refresh mood;
When you walk through hilly tracks
The negativity of the mind brakes;
Going on foot through dense forest
Cautious mind always stay abreast;
Hiking never pollute water and air
Walking with friends is pleasure and fair.

All wives are same

Why all wives are same
Husband always to blame
Greed for name and fame
Scold husband if he became lame
Hide and seek is regular game
Neither can be easily tame
Each will say other shame, shame
But fight together for family name
All wives of world are same.

I can move alone

When no one comes to wipe my tears
I throw away my all the fears
In this world for me no one cares
So with the bottle I shout cheers;
My tears dry with the breeze
I take out ice from my freeze
Friends come to give accompany
Together they make only cacophony;
In the world we born alone with a cry
For surviving alone we must try
During rosy days everyone will say hello hi
In trouble time near and dear one also say bye;
I am used to walk alone in the madding crowd
This attitude allows me to move forward
Loneliness taught me not to become coward
Journey with others are lifetime award.

Love

You don't know when you may fall in love
You may get attracted to any curl and curve
No barrier of language, religion can stop
Caste, creed, colour, power all it can mop
Love is the binding force of male and female
In the modern society now love is for open sale
Yet love is viral and anyone can cheer and hail.

Enjoy your money

In the mad run for money
We come across leaving honey
Life is not a destination but journey
Every day is a beautiful tourney
So also the journey is funny;
When we run for money hunt
Our vision become very blunt
Time moves fast with money accumulation
When we realise the truth no solution
Poor health forced just face humiliation;
Honeymoon never lasts too long
Though your wealth may grow strong
So stop at every beautiful station
Eat honey with friends with satisfaction
Enjoying money than accumulation is better solution.

Why world is round?

God made this world round
So that we can hear his sound
Sunshine everybody can found
Air and water flow around
To him we are duty bound;
The world has no length and breadth
But every moment we have to breathe
The life in the world is complex math
Only few can gather money and wealth
The best can survive long with health.

Man Animal Conflict

With felling of plant and trees
Man animal conflict increase
The oxygen in air decrease;
Man destroyed trees and forests
They never think about animals interests
Thus converted many places to deserts;
Animals are not responsible for climate change
They always remain within natural range
Conflict with animal, man always arrange;
Man has expedite global warming
So ice of glaciers are quickly melting
Environment and ecology man only destroying.

Be like Quark

O' thy young Turk
On earth leave your mark
Be strong like shark
Ignite life with a spark
Overcome the dark
Give yourself a jerk
Make world beautiful park
Be like quark
No need to bark.

Think Logically

Why sacrifice animal for God
For this act he will not give nod
Don't hit the helpless with iron rod
Animals are beautiful tiny tod;
God is omnipotent and merciful
All over the universes he rule
Pleasing him by blood wrong tool
Human is making itself a fool
Think with logic when brain is cool.

Tik Tok

Tik tok tik tok
Life is full of flip flop
Up down up down
Silence and sound
Day and night comes
Round and round
Happiness and misery
Everywhere to found
Rise and fall come and go
Sometimes fast sometimes slow
Kiss and miss part of life
Joy and sorrow together strive
Tik tok tick talk
Your dance upload and unlock.

O' my sweetheart darling

O' my sweetheart darling
You are my Pound Sterling
Don't do bouncer balling
In fear my heart is falling
Please stop today's scolding;
Without you, life is vacuum
You are my companion premium
In my life you are like platinum
Sing a song with your harmonium
Don't force me to take opium.

I am defeated by destiny

Destiny forced me to kneel down
Once I had on my head golden crown
I was declared as a great hero
But in the final battle I became zero
My power, kingdom everything vanished
To solitary confinement I was banished
Power, money, might, glory all temporary
Only my shadow was my contemporary
Alexander, Napoleon, Hitler ends tragically
They are also the governed by destiny basically.

I love my Country

When I love my country
I can love the world
Human values automatically unfold;
Patriotism is not for sale
It is not to show and tell
Conduct will ring the bell;
He who don't love motherland
He can't help mankind
Such people are born blind;
Charity begins at home
Google has given us chrome
For humanity no need of bomb;
Love your family, love your neighbour
Your country you will love forever
One day you will be humanity's savour.

Die with Friendship

Whatever big palace you built
One day in the history it will tilt
Your stay in the palace is limited
To remove you, time is committed
To the graveyard you will be submitted;
Better sleep is important than palace
You may end up in hospital cold storage
Your palace may go to reverse mortgage
Better invest in health and relationship
Dine, wine, travel, dance and die with friendship.

Gandhi

He was a votary of peace
To India nonviolence teach
Cleanliness his beach
Love all he always preach
In world immortality he reach;
Gandhi was Buddha's true disciple
His life was honest and simple
India's independence was his mission
To wage war he never gave permission
Peace and nonviolence his submission;
He believed in religious tolerance
Division in the name of God nonsense
But flailed to induce people's common sense
India got Hindu-Muslim communal division
He was killed for a cause which was not his decision.

I like simple people

I like people who are simple
Of course, female with dimple
Simple people are honest people
In friendship they don't dribble
Their mindset is also not fickle;
Simple living gives them good health
High thinking is their real wealth
Beauty of world they can unfold
A batter new world they try to mould
Dignity and integrity, they always hold.

O God, lift your veil

When monkey lost its tail
It pushed all animals to jail
God's mercy to animals fail
Yet God didn't send a mail
Nor send a letter through rail
So to God, animals never hail
Many species lost their trail
God's own creation about to derail
The world man alone can't sail
Time is ripe for God to lift his veil.

Alcohol

One peg good, two change mood
Three is food, four can be rude;
What a wonderful liquid alcohol
Everyday many people lost control;
Many lost their hard earned money
But they can't live without red honey;
Alcohol can make the wise funny
One can become bankrupt without penny;
For the weak minded alcohol is elixir
With hundreds brand they are familiar;
Alcohol has devotes more than religion
Whisky, brandy, wine make own opinion;
To resolve problems alcohol is not solution
Yet during trouble it is man's best companion.

Move on move on

Living in a dynamic universe
Don't try to become static
Momentum make life fantastic
Static things become rustic
He who moves on are iconic;
Money, youth, beauty all temporary
Forever you will not remain honorary
You are not a permanent functionary
Time may block your artery coronary
Better move on drinking Bloody-marry;
The earth never stopped its rotation
To move around sun is its destination
Momentum is its natural inclination
So to move on never show hesitation.

Sankardev

He was poet, philosopher and reformer
Ahead of time he was a dreamer
He introduced a caste less society
Classes less world was his polity
Thought of socialism before Marxism
His philosophy was universal humanism
Preach for wellbeing of dog, fox and donkey
Ask his followers to treat every creature carefully
His dream was a beautiful world with peace and equity
Whole life worked to develop society with positive mentality
Sankardev was a prophet par excellence
Let the world now learn from him tolerance.

I blame none for failure

I blame none for my failure
I have done mistakes is sure;
I got opportunity to choose
But due to idleness I lose;
Nobody forced me my path
Always I thought I am right;
Best suggestion I have ignored
My ego I never allowed to lowered;
I thought I choose the best option
Never tried for change and rotation;
Now when I become lame duck
Why should I blame others for the stuck;
I have to change my destiny of my own
No one will give his success to me on loan.

Never tell a lie

No one wants to die
Yet one day has to fly
Someone will cry
Someone will say bye
Someone will remain shy
But everyone will die;
Don't make life dry
To make it better try
Be a bold and smart guy
Never tell a lie
Smile and say everyone hi.

Continue your journey

Don't calculate pain and gain
Umbrella is there for rain
Calculation will push you to drain
Make smile your companion main
Life is always a combination chain;
To pick nectar of life move smiling
Forgetting death rise after falling
Journey may not be smooth sailing
In the race of life you may be trailing
In the long run your smile will be shining;
When life cry every moment for a penny
To move forward you will see options many
Look at others, life is really very funny
One day the bold and beautiful will be nanny
So no need to calculate, continue your journey

Knowing is not enough

Count your chicken before it hatch
Otherwise total will never match;
Failure is the pillar of success is true
Provided from failure you take a clue;
The journey will start with a single step
But fill your fuel tank before you leap;
Practice leads to perfection you know
One day performance you must show;
Slow and steady wins the race
Provided no competitor is in haste;
Knowing a thing is not the actual fact
To achieve it with persistence you must act.

Namghar
(Assamese prayer house)

Not like Church, Mosque or temple
Namghar is an unique example
Combination of art, culture and spirituality
Shankardev established it scientifically
Namghar integrates people socially;
The seniors get respect on first row
To love and care children all devotes know
The unwritten conduct every one follow
The rhythm of prayer together flow
Let world see it's spirit and say wow.

Namghosa (নামঘোষা)

The gem of spiritual literature
The teaching of Namghosa is forever
Its philosophy is the tallest tower
Sing it's hymn in everyday prayer
Such a religious text in world is rare;
Namghosa teaches universal brotherhood
Work with denunciation for mankind's good
Even to the weakest one never become rude
Pray the sage who even don't desire salvation
Working with prayer for better world is best satisfaction.

Shankardev the unifier

When Assam's society was divided
Unification path Shankardev provided
All caste, creeds he tactfully united
Assamese identity to world enlightened;
Shankardev was not merely a spiritual guru
He laid foundation for Assam's better tomorrow
The best teachings of all religions he borrow
So his thinking and philosophy is not narrow;
God is omnipotent and expression less
Rituals and animal sacrifice to get him is useless
Purity of mind and soul can only bless
Through brotherhood and love society can progress.

Never stop momentum

The sun never rises or sets
Earth only moves on it's axis
We say Sunset on relative basis;
When sun sets in one place of earth
In some other places for light no dearth
The rotation of earth continues on it's path;
Never stop your momentum when it is dark
Otherwise you will lost your destination park
Time will give you untimely dead mark.

Logic and wisdom

A bird in hand is better than two in bushes
To catch them never make rushes;
The distant hill is always look beautiful
Going near you can see bump plentiful;
Never neglect near one for distant glamour
When you reached, will know all are rumour ;
If you can catch fish sitting on the sea shore
No need to go to the hostile mid sea any more;
Courage and confidence does mean blind move
Better success logic and wisdom will prove.

Don't sacrifice the innocent for God

Why sacrifice innocent animal
Why halal desert friend camel
Dog, fox, donkeys soul is also God
Sacrificing them for God is a fraud
To kill them God has not given his nod;
Shankardev taught futility of sacrifice
His salvation philosophy is precise
Pray God with clean and open mind
In animals also omnipotent you will find
So to the nature and earth always be kind;
The rituals are creation of vested people
With prayer, meditation live a life simple
God doesn't have a shape or bodily existence
He is infinite, shapeless and only to feel his omnipotence
For a better world, against sacrifice always give resistance.

Trust

Trust is very rare
So to trust be fair
It is also very fragile
Quickly become hostile
Trust is always volatile
Never static but mobile
To develop need year
Disappear in small fear
Be trustworthy for all
From top you will not fall
When people trust you
They will accept your view.

Loneliness

No one in this world alone
We are made of same clone
Loneliness is state of mind
Companion is easy to find
When we love the near and dear
As companion they will cheer
Selfishness always generates fear
In loneliness you have to shed tear
When you throw ego and greed
To your call everyone one will heed
Sing a song with birds under a tree
From loneliness you are always free.

Tentative Existence

Nobody knows how long he will live
So share with others when you are alive
Enjoy others smiling face when you give
People's small mistake always forgive
In this world nobody is permanent native;
Eat, drink and enjoy as much as you can
But be generous to others like a good man
Unused resources you can't take to grave
Everything you gather you have to leave
Your existence in this world is tentative.

Save sea from pollution

In human life cycle sea is equally important
The world is unique creation of omnipotent
Sea alone is bigger than all the continent
Living thing started at sea is also pertinent
To save sea from pollution is commitment
The vastness of sea inspires to think beyond
So once upon a time America was found
People realized long back world is round.

When heart beats increase

When my heart beat increases in fear
I know to help me God will be very near
To his children he is always kind and dear
With his presence I can wipe out my tears
I can move in life's path again on top gear;
In the darkest night with you God is there
Your sorrow and pain he will try to share
His absence during bad days is rare
When you pray he will certainly take care
To come near you he never asks taxi fare.

Listen to your Heart

Always listen to your heart
In trouble time it never flirt
To understand heart is an art
It can only clean mind's dart
Self-esteem it will not hurt;
Brain is too much logical
Gain and lose is mathematical
Anger is haste and surgical
Love is fragile and emotional
In confusion don't be political;
Heart is clear and transparent
Never think anything apparent
For the heart don't be deterrent
In darkest day heart is supplement
The path of heart is omnipotent.

Love is Reciprocal

Love and hate both are reciprocal
They are also apparently sinusoidal
But jealousy is always colonial;
Love follow Newton's third law
If you love someone they also follow
Hate also rebound with a blow;
The world is a place of action and reaction
Life and death forever move in continuation
So live and let live is the only solution;
Good action can create only reaction good
Honesty and trust creates pleasant mood
With ease you can digest your daily food.

Midnight Sun

When sweet heart ask for sun in midnight
You must realize that she wants to fight
Please accept that your pent will be tight
Better go out to search for Firefly's bright
Inside you can't win even applying might;
In the morning when the sun rises
You will have to listen to her cries
She will not ask for sun in the noon
Any moment sweetheart may ask for moon
Run for office before she throws a spoon.

Mba

MBA degree can't make an entrepreneur
For many students it remains as souvenir;
To become a successful businessman
One needs to be a hardworking human;
Positive attitude is important than capital
To do networking one should be social;
Keep eyes and ears open with close mouth
Always be prepared to travel north to south;
Meeting people with smile order of the day
To innovative and new idea no never say;
Learn from mistakes when you move forward
Knowledge, experience, wisdom gives best reward.

Degree

Don't be mad for a degree
Success will give it free
Follow passion with dedication
Give importance to innovation
To a problem find easy solution
You can make own institution
When equipped with best skill
The importance of degree is nil
With new idea work with will
In three hours exam no thrill.

Religion

Religion is a tool for division
God has not made this provision
It was only selfish man's creation
Now mankind need it's substitution
Accepting humanity is the solution;
Religion has no scientific basis
All religion has different thesis
For religion world is now in crisis
One day religion will be nemesis
Division of people let us resist.

Diwali

Diwali may be festival of light
But the pollution is not right
For a clean Diwali let us fight
Sound is not for showing might
Crackers causes only plight;
Light a lamp for better tomorrow
Burning hands will bring sorrow
For own interest safety rule follow
Don't ignite rockets to move like arrow
Harming nature will make Diwali narrow.

Why we wakeup

We wake up in the morning for breakfast
After eleven O' clock it will not last
Breakfast is the only attraction to rise
Otherwise sleeping with blanket is nice
Dreams of night fade in the morning
In the stomach hunger starts burning
Morning is also the time for pursing
Bread, butter, jam all are waiting
Wakeup don't miss the breakfast timing
In the office boss is ready for shouting.

Corruption in India

Corruption is Indian people's lifeline
Without corrupt money we can't dine
With bribe money God also shine
Between honesty and corruption no line
For the society corrupt people are fine;
We bribe God to give us instant favour
But reluctant to do necessary labour
Siphoning people's money we get honour
Nation is legacy of hypocrisy and clamour
To defy law Indian minds full of armour;
No leader can make India corruption free
Corruption in India is deep rooted tree
For us corrupt money is tastier than ghee
Struggle for a honest society is below knee
For a better India we have to bribe Thee.

False promise

Right-wing politicians can't eradicate corruption
For a corruption free society we need Revolution
Democracy and election is not a good solution
Corrupt people should be sent for execution
Tough law is needed with full proof implementation
For this society must unite with firm determination
Democracy is giving Indian people only lip service
For decades all politicians are giving us false promise.

O' Lord, Open your eyes

God is dumb, deaf and blind
But people say he is very kind
Our mistakes he never mind
So cruel man everywhere we find
Now is the time for God to unwind;
O' God open your eyes to see your creation
Seeing the world you will not get satisfaction
Listen to men's cruel and destructive international
You will be forced to speak out a new solution
Otherwise you will have to decide for mankind's destruction.

We are moving towards hunger

World is in Putin-Biden octopus trap
Changes will be in the world map
Indifferent people are still in nap
Some mad leaders are singing rap
Putin-Biden worried about winning cap;
Time for world leaders to think rationally
Otherwise, our lives will endanger seriously
Now is the time to resolve problems mutually
Economies are moving to recession actually
Hunger and poverty will engulf mankind suddenly.

UN is now silent spectator

United Nation is now a silent spectator
Leaders of nations are working as dictator
In deep sleeping, United Nation's solicitor
To bring disputing parties to talk, no mediator
All nations are ignoring peace and human factor;
Once the nuclear volcano erupts, no one can stop
Forever the United Nation will become a big flop
The so-called supreme animal will fall from the top
World leaders, contribute positive to mute war pop
To clean the mess after nuclear war, there will be no mop.

Uncertainty Principle

"If I am here, understand that I am not here
If I am not here, understand that I am here"
I am the soul of the everything, matter or non matter
For me only, infinite galaxies are everywhere
Without me all living beings will be no where;
From mother's womb, you change from child to old
Nothing was, is and will be in your hands to hold
Even your death is uncertain, always untold
Your position and momentum uncertain in my fold
So, move on, move on, in search of truth, the only gold.

Quantum entanglement

Proton, neutron, and electron not the ultimate end
New particles have given new twists and bend
If Quantum entanglement is a reality
We are certainly part of a singularity
Our physical existence is only irregularity;
Concept of entanglement for generations may not be myth
Our physical world will be in different bandwidth
Traveling in the speed of mind may become reality
Study of classical physics will be futility
Unified theory of everything can only give cosmological solidarity.

Genetic code

Sometimes I doubt human DNA and genetic code

Without bad gene, how humanity can so much erode

No school, college ever taught how to do corruption

To teach ragging, dowry not in syllabus of institution

Criminal mentality and criminal instinct beyond solution;

All schools and colleges teach integrity and honesty

But everywhere in the society, there is lack modesty

Parents never say their children to cheat in examination

But to uphold trust and fair play, problem of every institution

For a better new world, we need genetic code correction.

We are Paranormal

We are as insignificant as any other animal

Existence of billions and billions of stars is formal

Our existence in cosmos is very nominal and dismal

Existence of advanced civilization is quite normal

The living beings there may not be like mammal;

In comparison to advanced civilization, me may be decimal

They might be absorbing energy in the form of thermal

Their way of living and social behaviour may be optimal

For advanced civilizations, we may be funny and abnormal

Even in true sense, human beings are paranormal.

Discrimination a global phenomenon

Racial conflict is an old global phenomenon
To keep own race intact it was the cannon
Conflict for colour, creed, religion was common
Language and food habits also conflicts reason
Even within one country, discrimination to some region;
There is discrimination within the same colour and creed
This is because of human beings selfish need
Even within the same religion too much conflicts
Those people can also be called as racists
Even in twenty first century, discrimination persists.

By-product of Discrimination

The boundary disputes are by product of racism

No one wishes to live as rainbow pluralism

Though we say one country under one flag

But inside the country we quarrel for own tag

Even in same state one tribe pulls another's leg;

The evolution sociology is complex due to struggle for survival

To survive, tribes always tried to come out with strong revival

To maintain supremacy and protect land, tribes became rival

The racial discrimination always comes with new revival

Humanity as whole must try for discrimination removal.

Rapists need Encounter of third kind

They need close encounter of third kind
By the society, they can be easily find
For the encounter no one should mind
The legal system is clumsy and blind
Close encounter of third kind let's unwind;
Mother should not shed tears for rapist
Because their rapist offspring is racist
In the upbringing of rapists there is fault
Through encounter, the virus we must halt
For victim, rapist's free movement add salt.

Abortion of Female Foetus

Abortion of female foetus in India is still common
We must stop this dangerous social venom
Law is there to stop this crime and social evil
But some people are dangerous than devil
Greedy doctors are doing this job with zeal;
Rape, abortion of female foetus are social issue
There are people who encourage sati system for virtue
Wife beating by senior policeman is real and true
Brides lost their lives for dowry without any clue
The new generation will remove nexus of socio-religious glue.

Male chauvinism is age old

Male chauvinism is age old culture
Towards humanity it works like vulture
Even in family girls have to accept torture
Rape in society is a cancerous tumour
Gender equality is still a distant future;
Religion chauvinism supported by religion
Society is not willing to fight this opinion
Law alone can't give a permanent solution
From ages women are forced to prostitution
We need a different type of socio-cultural revolution;
Male chauvinism can't be changed only by education
It requires a long-term process of evolution
Male ego of superiority needs now humiliation
Gender equality should be civilized society's resolution
Let's stop rape, the worst form of crime and discrimination.

Rape

Rape is worst form of crime
Yet it survived for long time
Attitude of male is cause prime
It has no place in civilized society
We must make rape an old history;
Kings, powerful raped too many women
Female was commodity in their fiefdom
In democracy women have equal freedom
But rapist get punishment seldom
To eradicate rape, society need wisdom;
Rapists are brutal beasts and cowards
Capital punishment should be their rewards
The law against rape is seems to be tough
But punishing the guilty is not enough
Against rape society must be very rough.

Technology for better tomorrow

Technology is for better tomorrow
Don't use technology for sorrow
Vision of technology is not narrow
Without discrimination it allows to borrow
Always move forward technology's arrow;
Technology is not for destruction
It is to facilitate better construction
For human problems it gives solution
Hiroshima is blunder and aberration
Technology is not for humanity's humiliation.

Work life Balance

Balanced food alone not enough for good health

Food with exercise can give you valuable wealth

We earn money for comfort and better sleep

With good health you can dream of sleeping deep

A voyage in luxury ship with poor health is bad trip;

Good health can give opportunity for work and life balance

Together all will improve happiness and your tolerance

For a better new society, tolerance has great importance

Give more importance in health than materials substance

For new approach to life, mind will always give resistance.

Need and Greed

Life has given me what I need
Why should I feel sad for my greed
Greed creates jealousy, a bad breed
It is the right time mind should be freed
Got food cloth shelter and a happy family
Indian Oil gives medical support easily
When in job we need promotion
Now realised those were useless emotion
This is the best time to contribute for society
In Indian Oil we had worked for nation with sincerity
When we cry for others, greed disappear with tears
God gives us bonus to serve many healthy years.

Population

Every time I think for a solution
One word always disturbs me 'population'
India has thousands of problem
Nobody knows how to solve
Poverty, illiteracy, corruption
Caste, religion what will do government
Population is eating out all development
Unemployment is off shoot of population
One Day nation will go to hibernation
The worst sufferer shall be new generation.

About the Author

Devajit Bhuyan

DEVAJIT BHUYAN, Engineer, Advocate, Management & Career Consultant, was born at Tezpur, Assam, India, on 1st August, 1961. He completed Bachelor of Engineering (Electrical), from Assam Engineering College and subsequently completed Diploma in Industrial Management, from International Correspondence School, Mumbai, LL.B. from Gauhati University, Diploma in Management from Indira Gandhi Open University, and Certified Energy Auditor Examination from Bureau of Energy Efficiency (BEE), New Delhi. He is also a Fellow of the Institution of Engineers (India), Life member of Administrative Staff College of India (ASCI) and Assam Sahitya Sabha. He is having 22 years' experience in Petroleum and Natural Gas Sector and 16 years in education management. He has authored 70 books published by different publishers namely, Pustak Mahal, V&S Publishers, Spectrum Publication, Vishav Publications, Sanjivan Publications, Story Mirror, Ukiyoto Publishing etc. To know more about him please visit www.devajitbhuyan.com

www.ingramcontent.com/pod-product-compliance
Lightning Source LLC
LaVergne TN
LVHW041911070526
838199LV00051BA/2584